Sleeping Beauty

Adapted by Amanda Askew
Illustrated by Natalie Hinrichsen

Silver Dolphin
San Diego, California

Long ago, there lived a king and queen who had a beautiful baby girl.

The king could not contain his joy. He held a great feast and invited friends, family, and the fairies.

There were thirteen fairies in his kingdom.
All but the thirteenth fairy were invited,
because she was cruel and spiteful.

After an amazing feast, each of the fairies presented the child with a magical gift, including kindness and beauty.

The princess had everything she could wish for.

After the eleventh fairy presented her gift,
the thirteenth fairy suddenly appeared.

Angrily, she called out, "When she is fifteen years old, the princess shall prick herself with a spindle and fall down dead!"

The queen fell to the floor, sobbing.

The twelfth fairy, whose wish was still unspoken, quietly stepped forward.

"My magic cannot break the curse," she said. "But your daughter shall not die. Instead she will fall into a deep sleep lasting one hundred years."

Over the years, the fairies' promises
came true, one by one.

The princess grew to be beautiful...

kind...

and wise.

The king and queen ordered every spindle across the kingdom to be destroyed. The princess was never told of the curse.

On the morning of her fifteenth birthday, the princess awoke early, excited. She wandered through the halls and gardens, waiting for the rest of the castle to awake.

She came to an old tower that she had
never seen before. The princess climbed the
winding staircase and opened a little door.

In a small room sat an old woman with a spindle, busily spinning.

"What are you doing?" asked the princess.

"I'm spinning," said the old woman.
"Would you like to try?"

The princess had hardly begun when she pricked her finger. At that moment, she fell into a deep sleep.

The king, queen, and servants had all started their
morning routines when they suddenly fell asleep, too.

The horses fell asleep in the stable...

the birds fell asleep on
the roof...

and the dogs snored in
the yard.

Around the castle a thick hedge of roses grew, until nothing could be seen of the castle.

The legend of Sleeping Beauty, as the king's daughter was called, spread across the land. Princes tried to reach the castle, but the thorns would not let them through.

One hundred years passed, and a handsome young prince heard the tale of Sleeping Beauty. He traveled to the castle and walked through the hedge unharmed.

When he went into the castle, the flies were asleep on the walls and the servants were asleep in the halls.

Near the throne lay the king and queen, sleeping peacefully beside each other.

At last, the prince reached the tower where
the princess slept. As soon as he saw her, the
prince fell in love. He bent down to kiss her,
and Sleeping Beauty awoke.

The sleeping curse was lifted, and the castle
slowly came to life.

Later that year, the prince and Sleeping Beauty were married and lived happily for the rest of their lives.

Notes for parents and teachers

- Look at the front cover of the book together. Can the children guess what the story might be about? Read the title together. Does this give them more of a clue?

- When the children first read the story, or you read it together, can they guess what might happen at the end?

- What do the children think of the characters? Is the thirteenth fairy kind? What about the king and queen? Who is their favorite character, and why?

- The villain in this story is the thirteenth fairy. Can the children think of any other stories with a similar character?

- At the beginning, do the children think that Sleeping Beauty will fall asleep for one hundred years? How do the children feel when the prince breaks the curse at the end of the story?

- What would the children do if they met an evil fairy? Ask the children to draw or paint their own nasty character.

- What other endings can the children think of? Ask the children to act out the story, and then the new endings.

- Many princes try to help Sleeping Beauty, which is very kind. What things do the children do for other people that are kind? Why is kindness important?

Silver Dolphin Books
An imprint of the Baker & Taylor Publishing Group
10350 Barnes Canyon Road, San Diego, CA 92121
www.silverdolphinbooks.com

Copyright © QEB Publishing, Inc. 2010

ISBN-13: 978-1-60710-348-6
ISBN-10: 1-60710-348-6

Manufactured, printed, and assembled in Guangdong, China.
1 2 3 4 5 15 14 13 12 11

The Library of Congress has cataloged the original QEB edition as follows:

Askew, Amanda.
  Sleeping Beauty / as told by Amanda Askew.
     p. cm. -- (QEB storytime classics)
  Summary: A retelling of the traditional tale in which a wicked fairy, enraged at not being invited to the princess' christening, casts a spell that dooms the princess to sleep for one hundred years.
  ISBN 978-1-59566-791-5 (library binding)
  [1. Fairy tales. 2. Folklore--France.] I. Sleeping Beauty. English. II. Title.
  PZ8.A91Sl 2010
  398.2--dc22
  [E]
                                                    2010005387

Editor: Amanda Askew
Designers: Vida and Luke Kelly